FC DREAMS:
Out of Time

M. AREAUX

Copyright

Fortnite Dreams is a work of fiction. All names, characters, locations, and incidents are the products of the author's imagination or are used fictitiously. Any resemblance to actual events, locales, or persons, living or dead, is entirely coincidental.

Editing by KP Editing
Cover Design by bobooks
Published by Kingston Publishing Company
- www.kingstonpublishing.com

Table of Contents

Dedication

For two little boys who dream big, imagine adventures, and love magically; this book is for you.

Chapter 1

Knock-knock.

I looked up from my television as the sound echoed through my headset. I place my favorite camo colored controller onto my nightstand, pausing my game of Fortnite. I was talking with some of my other friends as we all battled a mission together on my favorite game, Fortnite.

Ugh, not again. I hated being interrupted when I was playing my games. But, I learned my lesson the hard way not to argue about playing games. I had also learned that the people around me were more important than a video game. Well, most of the time anyway.

I knew who it was before I even opened the door. Ever since I had told my best friend, Cooper, about my time in the Fortnite game, he was rushing at the chance to come over and play the game with me.

He had this wild idea that if he played Fortnite at my house, that he too, might find himself inside the video game.

As cool as it was getting to meet my favorite characters and see all of the awesome places in the game, I still wasn't sure if it had been real, or just a wild dream.

Cooper was the only person who I had told, and I planned on keeping it that way.

"Connor, come on, let me in," Cooper yelled from the other side of my door.

Rolling my eyes, I got up off my chair and opened the door.

A very eager looking Cooper was standing in front of me.

"Hi, Cooper," I said, as I turned and went back to my comfy, oversized chair.

Following me inside the room, Cooper began talking so fast, it was hard to understand what he was saying.

"Did you hear season ten just came out? I heard it has Gotham City in it!" Cooper shouted, as a big smile spread across his face.

"Yeah, I know. I am downloading the game now," I said, pointing to my screen. The Season eleven logo was on the screen; a circle with three triangles coming out the sides. Fortnite characters sat inside each triangle. It was so cool.

"I can't wait to play," Cooper began. Scooting closer to me and lowering his voice to a whisper, he began to talk again. "Do you think you will get trapped inside the game again?" he asked.

I jumped up and ran to close my bedroom door. Looking around, I held my hands up. "I told you not to talk about that," I warned.

"Come on, Connor. I am your best friend. Plus, how cool would it be if it happened again and I go to come with you too?" he asked, his eyes sparkling with interest.

I knew I had made a mistake telling Cooper about my dream as soon as the words came out. Ever since then, he has been asking me like a million questions.

"I don't even know if it really happened," I said.

"Sure you do. I believe you that it happened," Cooper said.

He was a great friend and had always been loyal to me, but to believe that I had actually been trapped inside a Fortnite game was almost too much for any best friend to believe.

"Look, my game is still downloading. How about you come over tomorrow after school and we can play?" I offered.

Cooper jumped up and down, stoked to get the chance to come back and play. He had his own XBox and could play the game at his own house anytime he wanted. However, he had it set in his mind that my game was magical or something like that. He truly believed that if he played the new season at my house, he could experience the same thing I had too.

After Cooper left that night, I ate dinner with my parents, finished my homework, and took the dog for a walk. Once I was finished with everything I had to do, I went back up to my bedroom and noticed the game was almost done downloading. I was so tired from my full day of school and chores that I could barely keep my eyes open.

The last thing I remember before falling asleep was the words- Download Completed- displaying across my television screen.

Chapter 2

"Connor, you need to get onto the 4-wheeler now," a deep, dark voice stated.

"Dad?" I asked, as I slowly opened my eyes. It didn't sound like my dad, but the voice was definitely from a guy. Had I overslept and missed the bus?

Just as the thought crosses my mind, I see a large blue battle bus soaring through the air. The gliders are deployed and they are preparing to land.

I rub my eyes again, not believing what I am seeing--again!

I turn to the figure who was talking to me. It is Batman!

And, I am standing in front of a large 4-wheeler-- not the Batmobile. The black 4-wheeler has sharp features, large wheels, and more glowing gadgets than a spaceship.

Oh no!

I did it again. I am in a Fortnite game.

But wait, I have never played this new season. The last time this happened, I had played the game in that season and terrain over a million times. I knew everything about where to hide and which characters to look out for. Now, I was going into this blindly with no experience to guide me.

How would I survive this?

"Connor, you need to get onto the 4-wheeler so we can get out of here," Batman urges.

His gloved hands are on the steering wheel and as he looks at me, I admire his black cape and suit, along with his black mask. He looks so cool and dangerous. I know I can trust Batman, he fights crime and saves the good guys.

Without giving it another thought, I jump onto the back of the 4-wheeler.

Running up to the car, with her signature bright purple hair, is Pixie.

"Hey, Connor. You are back," she says, as she jumps onto the back of the 4-wheeler behind me.

I don't have time to answer her when I am momentarily shocked by the scene outside the car.

This is a new town and a new place-- one I have seen before.

We are traveling through the streets of Gotham. Large buildings line the streets and as we pass by broken cars and smaller, old and rundown buildings, I take in the darkness of the area.

"What is going on?" I ask, finally able to find my words.

"Catwoman has created an army of robot zombies and she is trying to take over Gotham City," Batman says, as his deep voice fills the car.

As I sit in the passenger seat, the car speeding down the streets of Gotham City, I can't help but feel a mixture of excitement and dread.

I am trapped inside a Fortnite game.

Chapter 3

Why does this keep happening to me? All I want to do is play my favorite game and instead, I am now trapped inside the game.

Suddenly, the car stops and Batman and Pixie jump out. Without thinking, I get out of the car and follow closely behind them.

They run behind an old church and crouch down by a broken fence. I do the same and try to calm my breathing.

"What are we doing?" I whisper.

"Catwoman is hiding out in that building across the street," Batman says, pointing to a building that looks like it is about to fall down. Bricks lay scattered on the broken concrete sidewalk and windows are broken.

Reaching over, Pixie hands me a grenade.

"You know what to do with this," she smiles. "It's just like last time," she adds.

Gasping, I almost drop it, but thankfully, I manage to catch the grenade. I remain crouched down, unable to move as I look at the destructive weapon in my hands.

My heart began to beat rapidly like a drum and my legs shook. I felt like I might fall over, but Batman placed his hand on my shoulder.

"I know you are scared, but remember we must stop the bad guys from winning. Catwoman has a destructive army and if they take over Gotham, only evil and trouble will prevail," he says, looking me in the eye.

I know I have to help them, even if I am unsure about what I am doing. So, I launch the grenade toward the building. I watch the blast of bright oranges and reds light up the dark sky. The explosion knocks me off my feet and I fall onto the ground below with a thud.

As soon as the dust clears, hundreds of robot zombies begin pouring out of the old building. Half of the building has been knocked down, so they have an easy way to get out. Their green faces and silver armor make them look like they are from a horror movie.

"Good job," Batman says.

"Thanks," I say, still a little out of breath.

"Now we need to move," Pixie says, as she pulls me to my feet and we begin to run across another road. This part of Gotham is filled with smoke and the sky looks like a creepy gray. It almost looks like an abandoned town and I wonder if this is because of Catwoman.

The three of us begin to run down a long, alleyway and I can hear the steps of the robot zombies behind us. They must have spotted us.

"How many do you think are after us?" I ask, trying to keep up with Batman and Pixie.

"Hundreds," Pixie says, right before throwing a grenade over my head and at the zombies.

An explosion rocks the earth behind me and I almost fall down, but I keep running anyway.

Batman stops at a large, old building and opens a rusty, metal door.

We enter into the old building and race up a flight of stairs. We stopped in a room and close the door behind us. I spin around and face the wall and try to calm my rapid breathing. I can hear voices yelling just outside the building and I hope they stay outside. It's the zombies. They don't seem to know how to get inside. Maybe that's why zombies eat brains? They don't have any of their own, so they need human brains to think?

I laugh to myself at the thought. I walk around and suddenly, realization strikes me.

I have been here before!

This is the same building I came to last time I was trapped in Fortnite!

Chapter 4

Pixie peaks out a broken window and looks for any sign of the attackers. I smile to myself because for once, something feels familiar here. As I begin to inspect the room, I spot a chest in the far corner. The same chest I remember seeing the last time I was here. I rush to the chest and open the heavy lid.

Inside are several different types of weapons I have used in hundreds of missions in the Fortnite game. I grab as many as I can hold before I turn to Batman and Pixie.

"Hey guys, I found a chest. We need to grab some weapons," I yell to them.

Pixie turns to me with a wide grain. "Connor, you are doing so great. It's almost like you are leading the mission this time," she says.

Her words sink in and I can't help but feel really good knowing she approves of how I am doing. All I want to do is show them that I can handle this mission and to help them stop the bad guys. In my world, good always prevails and that's exactly what is going to happen here.

Chapter 5

Without warning, a large boom sounded from downstairs and then heavy footsteps bound up the stairs.

Oh no! The robot zombies have found a way inside to us.

"The zombies are coming," Batman says, in his deep, serious voice.

"How?" Pixie asks, running over to the window to look outside.

"Catwoman," is all Batman says.

I can honestly say, I didn't expect the next thing that happened.

But, when you are trapped in a Fortnite video game, I guess you really can't expect or be prepared for anything that happens.

After I had collected all of the weapons, we were instantly transported back to the lobby. The blue battle bus was waiting outside the lobby doors for us. I began to search the new map, even though my heart wasn't into it.

We had just started this mission. How could we have been eliminated and brought to the starting point?

Confused and feeling like I had failed, I sigh.

"How did this happen?" I ask, my voice filled with defeat.

"Don't get down on yourself," Batman says. "We haven't lost yet. We just had a glitch in our mission," he smiles.

I guess he is right. I mean, he is Batman. He knows best.

Pixie waves for us to follow her to the battle bus and we load up. As I step onto the bus, I pause as seated in almost every row, are guys with tomatoes for heads. They have green and red jumpsuits and all seem to be smiling at me. I shrug and load the bus anyway. This isn't the weirdest thing I have seen in Fortnite.

We fly high into the air and I am amazed by the bright blue sky and white, puffy clouds. Even though I have already experienced this before, it still amazes me seeing it again in person. Once we are high enough, we open the battle bus doors and jump out, extending our gliders.

When I take a second to look at my glider, I am amazed to see that it is a dragon glider. The dragon glider is blue and silver with frosted wings and I feel like I am a real dragon, flying high above the green grass below. I remember these frosted wings from previous seasons and I get excited that it has returned. Light blue water surrounds a tiny island. I spot Valykrie, Nite Nite, and Peekaboo flying around me.

The sky becomes dark purple and blue as we begin to approach the ground. I see a big crater with lots of trees and a broken-down facility. We are heading toward Dusty Divett. This is the same Dusty Divett I came to last time, but it looks really different. Snow covers the ground and small, white flakes swirl in the now frigid air. There is a large meteor hole here.

"Why does this look different?" I ask, as we all land onto the snow-covered ground.

"Catwoman is turning everyone around her evil. The tension was so much, that the orb at Loot Lake exploded. The time stream at the Island became disoriented. New landmarks were created and some older ones that were once eliminated have returned. The battle of good and evil has transformed this entire world. As more evil grows in troops, the Fortnite world will begin to destroy itself," Pixie states, her voice filled with sadness.

If we don't stop evil now, the entire Fortnite world could be destroyed forever.

Chapter 6

Standing in the frozen destruction zone that was once Dusty Divett, I spot troops of futuristic cowboys running with cowboy hats and long, trench coats. They have sparks of white light shooting out of their hands and weapons. It is so cool looking, but I have to react fast and remind myself I am on a mission.

"Connor, we need to get to a safety zone," Pixie yells over the thunder of the troops heading our way. Out of the corner of my eye, I spotted several other people running in the same direction as we are.

Each skin is different from the next characters. Everyone is trying to survive and our answer is only a few meters away. The battle has begun and if the three of us don't find a way to help the good guys and stop Catwoman and her evil robot zombies... I can't even finish the thought.

We all reach the circle at the same time, but only a few of us can fit inside. Thankfully, Pixie and I make it to the center and watch as those who weren't fast enough vanish before our very eyes. I feel bad for them, but I am also relieved to know that they will respawn soon into a new match.

Pixie, Batman, and I wait as our health rebuilds and once we are back up to a normal healthy level, we jump out of the circle and begin our search for another good hiding place where we can set up a mission.

"Once we find safety, we need to devise a plan to stop Catwoman, and now," Batman states firmly.

A guy in a clown suit and another with a long, white beard sees us and waves.

"Are you trying to stop Catwoman," the clown man asks.

"Yes," Pixie yells back to him.

"You need to hide behind that old building," the bearded man says. "We have been harvesting tools back there. You can use them along with your weapons," he finishes.

We see an old building with heavy bricks and we all nod in agreement that we need to find safety there. I begin digging into the ground along with Pixie and Batman. We find axes, shovels, and hammers that we can use to protect ourselves. Along with our grenades and bombs secured from the chest, we are good with weapons.

"We need a plan and we need one now," Pixie rushes out. "We can't be out of time yet."

"Those robot zombies can only think when they are being told what to do. We need to eliminate them first. Catwoman is using them to stop us," Batman states.

He holds up two large bombs and begins to prepare them for launching. Pixie and I close our ears as Batman throws the bombs toward the robot zombies still coming toward us.

The blast that follows knocks Pixie and me off our feet and sends us flying backward. We land onto the frozen ground below and my head begins to pound from the impact.

Pieces of zombie robots fly all around us. A heavy smoke fills the air and for some strange reason, silence takes over.

I no longer hear the heavy footsteps chasing us. I don't hear bombs exploding or voices yelling.

It's an eerie silence and I don't like it all.

Chapter 7

Pixie and I stand up, dusting ourselves off from the debris that is still falling from where Batman blew up the zombie robots. We look to one another and both smile when we see we are alright.

Our smiles quickly fade as we glance around and notice everyone is staring in the same direction. Even Batman.

Slowly walking out of a heavy fog, I spot Catwoman walking toward us. Her black catsuit glitters against the backdrop and her evil scowl makes her look more terrifying than most monsters. Above her, light flashes out of a large ship in the sky. The world around me remains still as we all wait and anticipate her next move. She moves carefully, knowing we are all anxious and nervous about what she is going to do.

From somewhere beside me, Batman slowly emerges. He begins to take long, slow strides toward Catwoman.

I want to yell out for him to stop. To tell him she is dangerous, but I know he is already aware of this. All I can do is watch and waite. Just like everyone else.

Once they come face-to-face, we all gasp as Catwoman holds her hands up into the air.

"Get out of the way, Batman. She is going to end you. There are more robots on their way. We can't let them win this match. This is our Fortnite Battle Royale!" a character in a cosmetic looking skin yells behind me.

His words remind me that I am a soldier in this crazy game. They also remind me that soldiers have to listen to their commanders. And right now, Batman is in charge here.

"Listen to what they say, Batman," Catwoman purrs, as she looks right at him.

"Your reign of terror ends now," Batman yells. "We are all prepared to do what it takes to stop you from bringing more evil into our world. Gotham is already falling apart. We will not allow you to bring any more evil to Fortnite," Batman finishes.

A volcano begins to erupt with orange and red lava flowing down the sides.

Catwoman swiftly turns and begins running toward the volcano. Batman chases after her and Pixie and I realize this is our chance.

We begin handing out the grenades, bombs, and the tools we have secured. Everyone takes their weapons and we all decide to go after Catwoman. Together.

We begin walking like an army, everyone in line as we march to the volcano.

As Catwoman makes her way to the top of the volcano, she turns and her evil smile fades as she realizes our army is coming for her. She had nowhere else to run and we can end her now or she can agree to leave this season forever.

A few of the skins throw grenades toward Catwoman. She is knocked off balance and almost falls into the raging, angry volcano that she is dangerously close to.

Fear paints her face and another bomb is thrown. This time, Catwoman falls to her hands and knees. She looks up stunned. She is surrounded by us and now she realizes she can't win.

"You have a choice to make now," Batman yells up to Catwoman. "You can leave now alive and agree to never return, or we will end you in this volcano."

He stands in front of us, his trusting army behind him.

Catwoman eyes all of us before she turns her attention to Batman.

The volcano is now shaking because of the lava still spewing out the side. We are all holding our weapons and ready to strike if needed.

With defeat lacing her voice, Catwoman calls down to us. "I will leave now, but this isn't over," she warns.

Shaking his head, Batman chuckles. "That's what you think."

Catwoman climbs down the side of the volcano and sprints away like the scaredy-cat she is.

Pixie begins to cheers as she raises her weapon in the air and begins to dance. Everyone around us follows in her excitement and starts celebrating.

Suddenly, a loud boom comes from up above us, high into the sky.

"VICTORY ROYALE," is announced, and the music begins to blare all around me like speakers suddenly were placed in this campsite.

Pixie and I smile as we begin dancing around like maniacs. I floss again, just like I did last time we won a match.

"I can't believe it, we won!" I cheer.

Batman walks over to us and I stop jumping around.

"Connor, thank you for helping us defeat Catwoman," Batman says. "I could really use a guy like you to help me defeat more bad guys in Gotham and our missions here in Fortnite," he finishes, smiling down at me.

Pride fills my heart and just as I go to respond, I hear a voice calling my name from behind me.

Chapter 8

"Connor, are you sleeping?"

My eyes shoot open and I jump up as I realize I had fallen asleep.

Standing in front of me is Cooper.

"What are you doing here?" I ask, wiping the sleep out of my eyes.

Laughing, Cooper looks down at me like I am crazy.

"Connor, it's morning. I came to see if you wanted to walk to school today. I was up last night watching our reruns of the Batman cartoons."

I glance around my room and notice the sunlight streaming in through my bedroom window.

"Wow, I guess I fell asleep waiting for Fortnite to download," I say.

The events all come back to me and as Cooper watches me carefully, he sees that I am remembering something, too.

"Did you say you were watching Batman?" I ask, laughter filling my voice.

"Yes," Cooper responds slowly. "Did it happen again?" he asks.

"I don't know what you are talking about," I say, trying to hide my wide smile.

I get up and begin getting my things ready for school. The entire time, Cooper is following me around, begging for details. I know I won't be able to keep this from him so I do the one thing that I know will make him happy.

"Let's head to school. I will tell you all about it," I say, looking back at my television screen.

41

The new season of Fortnite is displayed on the screen and I know without a doubt, that I was once again, trapped in a Fortnite world. I will never get tired of playing my favorite epic game and discovering what new and fantastic adventures I will embark on.

The End...Or Is It?